For Mom and Dad—M. J. D.

For Leo and Tommy—T. F. Y.

Published by Charlesbridge
85 Main Street
Watertown, MA 02472
(617) 926-0329
www.charlesbridge.com

Library of Congress Cataloging-in-Publication Data
Daley, Michael J.
Pinch and Dash and the terrible couch / Michael J. Daley;
illustrated by Thomas F. Yezerski.
p. cm.
Summary: When his aunt's couch is delivered to Pinch, he and
his friend Dash try to find a way to fit it into Pinch's cozy home.
ISBN 978-1-58089-379-4 (reinforced for library use)
ISBN 978-1-58089-380-0 (softcover)
1. Sofas—Juvenile fiction. 2. Dwellings—Juvenile fiction. 3. Animals—
Juvenile fiction. 4. Friendship—Juvenile fiction. [1. Sofas—Fiction.
2. Dwellings—Fiction. 3. Size—Fiction. 4. Animals—Fiction.
5. Friendship—Fiction.] I. Yezerski, Thomas, ill. II. Title.
PZ7.D15265Pf 2012
813.54—dc23
2011025704

Printed in Singapore
(hc) 10 9 8 7 6 5 4 3 2 1
(sc) 10 9 8 7 6 5 4 3 2 1

Illustrations done in pen and ink and watercolor on hot-press paper
Text type set in Adobe Caslon, display type set in Blue Century by T-26
Color separations by KHL Chroma Graphics, Singapore
Printed and bound September 2012 by Imago in Singapore
Production supervision by Brian G. Walker
Designed by Susan Mallory Sherman

Pinch and Dash
and the Terrible Couch

Michael J. Daley

Illustrated by Thomas F. Yezerski

✶ Charlesbridge

Pinch and Dash
and the Terrible Couch

Ding-Dong

Pinch sat in his snug chair.
He was reading a cookbook.
The doorbell rang.
Ding-dong.

5

Pinch ignored the bell.
He was lazy.
Ding-dong.
The cookbook was very good.
Ding-dong. Ding-dong!
DING-DONG!
The bell was hard to ignore,
even for a lazy person
with a good cookbook.

"Maybe it is Dash," Pinch thought.
"Maybe he wants
  to invite me to lunch."
He closed the cookbook.
He went to answer the doorbell.

Pinch opened the door.
A couch stood on his top step.
"Why is a couch ringing my bell?"
Pinch asked.
"The couch is not ringing your bell,"
said a voice. "I am."
The voice belonged to someone
standing in the flower bed.

"We saw you sitting in there,"
   said a second voice.
   It came from the other end
   of the couch.
"We rang and rang," said the first voice.
"What took you so long?"

Push and Shove

"Who are you?" Pinch asked.
"I am Push," said the first voice,
"and he is Shove. We are movers."

"We move things," Shove said.
"We do not stand around
  holding things."
"Right," Push said.
"So where do you want this couch?"

"I do not want it at all!"
  Pinch cried.
"Too bad," Shove said.
  Push and Shove carried the couch
  into the house.
"There must be some mistake!"
  Pinch cried.
"We are holding again," Shove said.

They carried the couch into the den.
"Look," Push said. "A fireplace."
"Just where a couch belongs,"
  Shove said.

"It will not fit!" Pinch cried.
"Sure it will," Push said.
   Push shoved the snug chair.

"No problem," Shove said.
   He pushed the desk.
   They put the couch down.
"This job is done," Push said.

"Wait!" Pinch cried.
"You cannot leave this couch here!"
"Give him the note," Shove said.
"Oh, right, I forgot," Push said.

"Note?" Pinch asked.
"Why didn't you give me
the note right away?"
"Well, we are movers, you know,"
Shove said. "Not mailmen."

Aunt Hasty in a Pinch

The movers left Pinch alone with the note and the couch.

Pinch read the note:

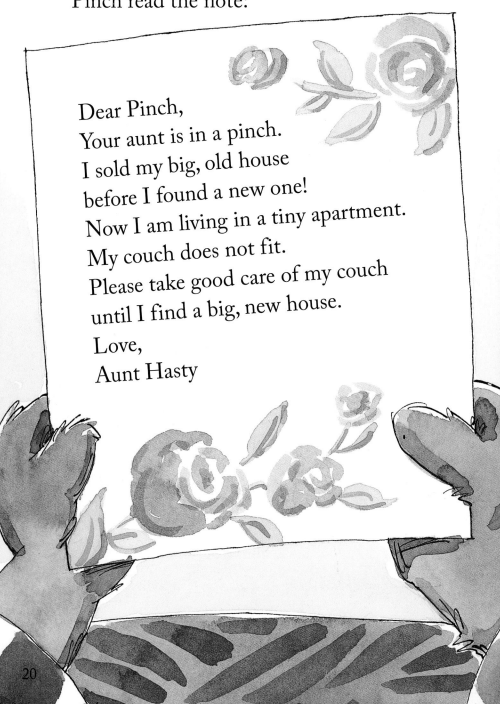

Dear Pinch,
Your aunt is in a pinch.
I sold my big, old house
before I found a new one!
Now I am living in a tiny apartment.
My couch does not fit.
Please take good care of my couch
until I find a big, new house.
Love,
Aunt Hasty

Pinch sank into his snug chair.
His knees bumped the wall.
The arm of the couch
poked his elbow.
His snug chair was not snug
anymore.

"Pinch? Oh, Pinch!" Dash called.
"Those movers left the door open.
A fly might get in."
Dash closed the door.
He stepped into the den.

"What a nice couch!" Dash cried.
"I love those daring dashes of red."

23

"This is a terrible couch," Pinch said.
"It is too large.
The cushions are too soft.
The colors do not match my curtains.
My curtains are blue.
They have pleasing pinches of orange.
I do not like daring dashes of red!"
Dash scratched his head.
"Pinch, why did you buy this couch?"
Dash asked.
"I did not buy this couch!" Pinch cried.
"I do not want this couch!"
Pinch handed Dash the note.

Hard Work

"**O**h, dear," Dash said.
"Maybe Aunt Hasty will want it back soon."

"No, she will not.
 She will decide to take a world tour,"
 Pinch said.
"She will decide she likes tiny apartments."

"I must agree," Dash said.
"Your Aunt Hasty is like that."
"She will forget about this couch," Pinch said.
"I will never sit in my snug chair again."
 Pinch sniffled.
"We can fix that," Dash said.

"Get up! Get up!
I love to rearrange furniture," Dash said.
"You take that end. Together now."

Pinch shoved.
Dash pushed.

"The couch is very heavy," Pinch said.
"Just a bit more," Dash said.
   They pushed and shoved some more.

"I am stuck," Pinch said.
"I cannot get out!"
"It needs to go against the other wall,"
   Dash said.

"I am tired of pushing and shoving,"
Pinch said.
"We need a lemonade break," Dash said.

Lemonade

Dash went into the kitchen.
"Oh, Pinch! There are no lemons.
I cannot make lemonade without lemons,"
Dash said.

Pinch said, "There is mix
in the cupboard. Use that."
"Mix!" Dash cried. "Mix tastes terrible.
There are lemons at my house.
I will be right back."
"Wait!" Pinch cried.
Dash left Pinch trapped in the corner
with the terrible couch.

Dash came back with tall glasses
full of ice and lemonade.
Pinch sipped.
He puckered.
He gulped.
"This lemonade needs a pinch more sugar,"
Pinch said.

Dash said, "No, no.
That pucker gives you pluck.
Now, let's move this couch!"

Dash pushed this way.
Pinch shoved that way.
They moved the desk and the snug chair.

They moved the table and the lamp.
Pinch cried, "I do not like
all this hard work!"

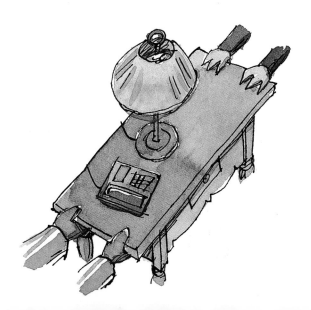

"Let's sit down," Dash said.

"We can rest before we try again."

He flopped onto the couch.

"Ahhh," Dash said.

"These cushions are just right for me."

Pinch sat down.

"My toes are in the fireplace!" Pinch cried.

"Zzzzzz," Dash said.

He was asleep.

Good-bye, Couch

$\mathbf{P}$inch was hot.
He needed some air.
Pinch opened a window.

The breeze was cool.
The breeze blew his curtains
with the pleasing pinches of orange.

It blew the curtains in Dash's house—curtains with daring dashes of red!

Pinch peeked at Dash.
Dash snored.
Pinch smiled.
Pinch tiptoed to the telephone.
He dialed.
"P and S Movers. Shove speaking,"
Shove said.
"Come to my house right away,"
Pinch whispered.
"I have a job for you."